NATIVE AMERICAN CULTURES

NATIVE AMERICAN HOMES

FROM LONGHOUSES TO WIGWAMS

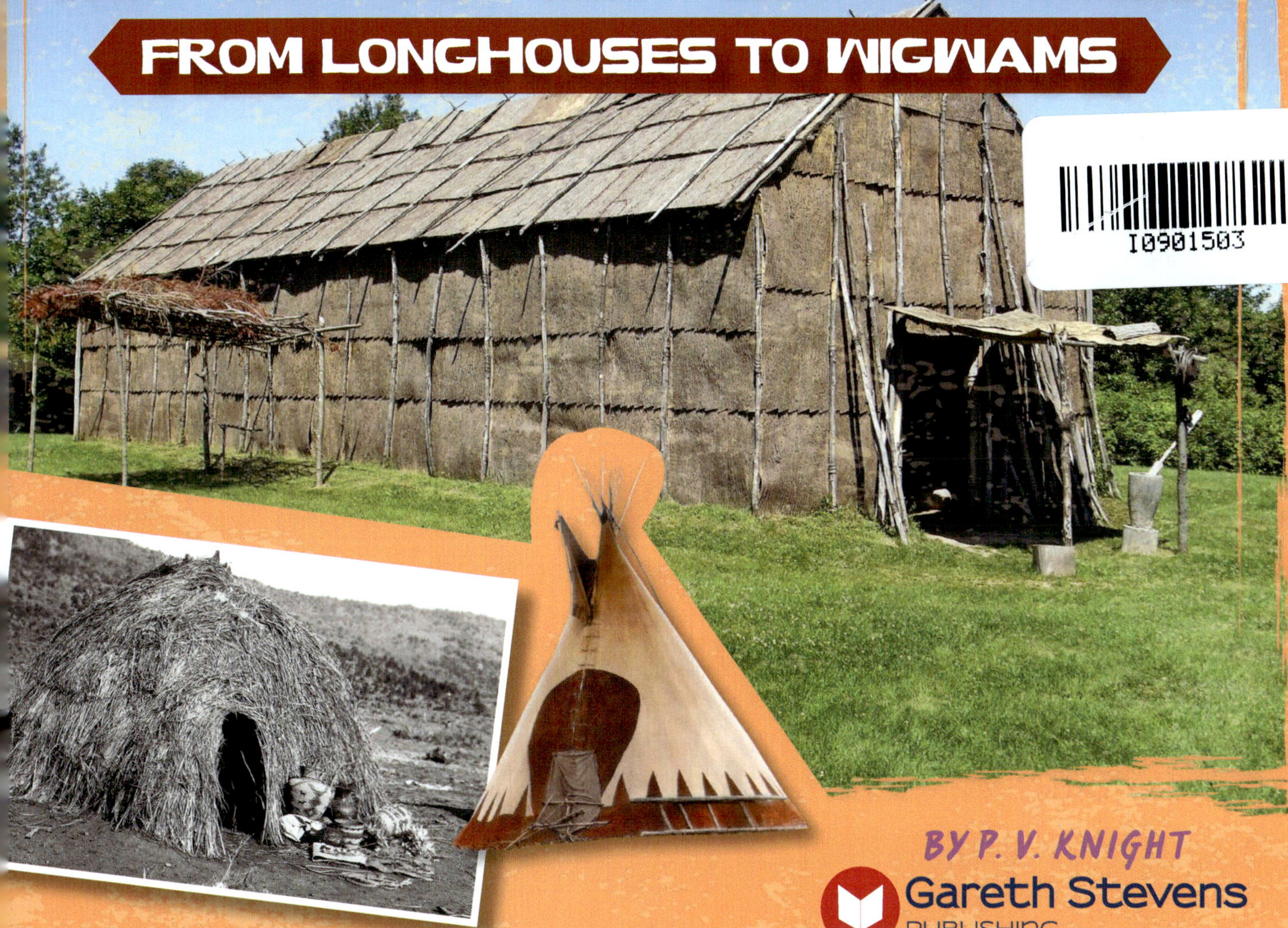

BY P. V. KNIGHT

Gareth Stevens PUBLISHING

Please visit our website, www.garethstevens.com. For a free color catalog of all our high-quality books, call toll free 1-800-542-2595 or fax 1-877-542-2596.

Cataloging-in-Publication Data

Names: Knight, P. V.
Title: Native American homes: from longhouses to wigwams / P. V. Knight.
Description: New York : Gareth Stevens Publishing, 2018. | Series: Native American cultures | Includes index.
Identifiers: LCCN ISBN 9781538208922 (pbk.) | ISBN 9781538208946 (library bound) | ISBN 9781538208939 (6 pack)
Subjects: LCSH: Indians of North America–Dwellings–Juvenile literature.
Classification: LCC E98.D9 K59 2018 | DDC 392.3'60899708–dc23

First Edition

Published in 2018 by
Gareth Stevens Publishing
111 East 14th Street, Suite 349
New York, NY 10003

Designer: Sarah Liddell
Editor: Therese Shea

Photo credits: Cover, p. 1 (main image) Paul Henry Beaumont/Shutterstock.com; cover, p. 1 (photograph) Brian0918/Wikimedia Commons; cover, p. 1 (tepee) Catfisheye/Wikimedia Commons; p. 4 Don Mammoser/Shutterstock.com; p. 5 Historical Picture Archive/Contributor/Corbis Historical/Getty Images; p. 6 MarmadukePercy/Wikimedia Commons; p. 7 Historical/Contributor/Corbis Historical/Getty Images; p. 8 Jeangagnon/Wikimedia Commons; p. 9 BotMultichillT/Wikimedia Commons; p. 10 Cortomaltais/Wikimedia Commons; p. 11 Marilyn Angel Wynn/Corbis Documentary/Getty Images; p. 12 Clive Streeter/Dorling Kindersley/Getty Images; pp. 13, 15 Marilyn Angel Wynn/Nativestock/Getty Images; pp. 14, 20 Fæ/Wikimedia Commons; p. 16 Greg and Jan Ritchie/Shutterstock.com; p. 17 Gooseterrain2/Wikimedia Commons; p. 18 Doug Meek/Shutterstock.com; p. 19 Angel McNall Photography/Shutterstock.com; p. 21 Josfer/Shutterstock.com; p. 22 Innotata/Wikimedia Commons; p. 23 FastilyClose/Wikimedia Commons; p. 24 Voltaire's Vaquero/Wikimedia Commons; p. 25 Nebakanezer/Wikimedia Commons; p. 26 AGF/Contributor/Universal Images Group/Getty Images; p. 27 boreala/Shutterstock.com; p. 29 Blend Images/Shutterstock.com.

Printed in the United States of America

CPSIA compliance information: Batch #CW18GS: For further information contact Gareth Stevens, New York, New York at 1-800-542-2595.

CONTENTS

Words in the glossary appear in **bold** type the first time they are used in the text.

HOME IS SHELTER

What does home mean to you? It likely means many things. It's the place you share with your family. It's where you eat meals and sleep. It's the place you **celebrate** special occasions. It's where you find **shelter** in bad weather and comfort after a bad day.

Home was all these things to Native Americans as well. But not all Native American homes looked alike. Different groups of Native Americans built different kinds of homes, depending partly on the **natural resources** around them.

MESA VERDE NATIONAL PARK IN COLORADO

Swiss artist Karl Bodmer traveled through the American West in the 1830s, creating pictures of the land and Native Americans. This print copies a picture Bodmer made of the inside of a Mandan Indian home.

HIDES, EARTH, SNOW, AND MORE

Native Americans used many kinds of natural resources to make their homes. Some groups used bison, or buffalo, hides. Some used trees, branches, bark, and grass. Others used earth and mud. Still others used **adobe** blocks and stone. And in the cold Arctic areas of the North, some used snow and ice!

A group's way of life also shaped Native American homes. Some groups lived in settled villages, while others were **nomadic** and needed homes they could carry with them.

The picture on the left shows the homes and crops in a settled Native American village in the East. The picture here shows the home used by nomadic Plains Indians, which was easy to set up, take down, and carry with them when they moved.

DID YOU KNOW?

Weather was an important consideration, too. It gets up to 100°F (38°C) in the Arizona desert and down to –50°F (–46°C) in Arctic areas!

TEPEES

The usual home of nomadic Plains Indians was the tepee, or tipi. It was a cone-shaped wooden frame with a covering made of 12 to 14 bison hides. The frame was made of 13 poles from 15 to 18 feet (4.6 to 5.5 m) long. The poles were stuck in the ground to form a circle about 12 to 16 feet (3.7 to 4.9 m) wide.

Tepees were women's work. Women prepared the poles and hides, made the hide covering, put up the tepees, and took them down.

DID YOU KNOW?

Since there would be a fire burning inside the tepee, there was an opening at the top to let smoke out. The door was a bison hide with the hair still on it or a bearskin.

Although a tepee was large enough for a whole family, it was easy to take down. An entire village could have tepees packed and ready to move within an hour.

LONGHOUSES AND WIGWAMS

WIGWAM

The Haudenosaunee (Iroquois) and Algonquian-speaking peoples lived in settled villages and wanted homes that would last a long time. Their homes were much alike except for their size. The Haudenosaunee built longhouses for many families to share. Algonquian-speaking peoples often built smaller homes called wigwams.

Longhouses and wigwams had a frame of poles and a curved, or arched, roof. Sheets of bark covered the frame and were tied in place. One or more holes in the roof allowed smoke from the fires to escape.

Some Algonquians covered their homes with grass mats, animal hides, or blankets instead of bark.

DID YOU KNOW?

The Haudenosaunee were known for their longhouses. In fact, "Haudenosaunee" means "people of the longhouse."

WATTLE-AND-DAUB HOUSES

Native peoples of the Southeast were farmers and hunters who wanted homes that would last a long time. They built what are called wattle-and-daub houses.

The term "wattle" has to do with the frame of the house. It was made of poles, or wattles, stuck into the ground, then **woven** with branches and **vines**. The word "daub" means the matter that was used to coat the frame. It was made with mud, clay, sand, **chalk** dust, dried grass, and even animal poop!

DID YOU KNOW?

The roof of a wattle-and-daub house was covered with grass, bark, or cane mats.

This picture shows a rebuilt Cherokee meeting house, which is a wattle-and-daub house. The picture on the left shows how the daub goes over the wattle frame.

CHICKEES

The Seminole Indians of Florida needed homes suited to the hot **wetlands** they lived in. So they built a special type of home called a chickee.

The chickee's frame was made of thick posts. The wooden floor was 3 to 4 feet (0.9 to 1.2 m) above the ground and was reached by a ladder. The pointed roof was made from palm leaves tied together with grass, rope, or vines. Walls weren't needed since it never got cold.

DID YOU KNOW?

The raised floor kept the Seminoles out of the mud, bugs, and snakes of Florida's wetlands!

When it rained, coverings of hide or cloth were put up along the sides to keep the rain out.

EARTH LODGES

Not all Plains Indians lived in tepees. Some were farmers who raised crops and needed homes that would last. They built strong, sturdy earth lodges.

The frame was made of 10 to 15 large posts arranged in a circle 20 to 50 feet (6 to 15 m) across. Four taller posts were set in the center. Beams were laid across the tops of the posts. Long poles with woven branches covered the beams. Then, hay and earth covered the whole thing. The entrance was through a short hall.

DID YOU KNOW?

An earth lodge was home to 15 to 25 people, along with favorite horses and dogs!

A hole was left in the roof to let light and air in and smoke out.

PUEBLOS

Native Americans in the desert Southwest were farmers. They built connected homes called pueblos (PWEH-blohz). The early ones were built of stone, but the later ones were built of adobe blocks, or bricks.

The stone pueblos were built of sandstone blocks held together with a mix of mud and water. The adobe pueblos had a frame of wooden posts and beams. Adobe bricks were laid around the frame and held together with a mix of mud and water.

DID YOU KNOW?

Each pueblo house had an entrance in the roof. It was reached by ladder.

Each family lived in a single room, although side rooms could be added if the family grew too large.

HOGANS

The Navajo of the desert Southwest didn't live in pueblos. They had moved to the Southwest from northern lands and brought a different style of housing with them. They lived in houses called hogans.

To build a hogan, the Navajo first dug a **shallow** pit in the ground. Then they set up a frame using posts made from the piñon pine tree. Finally, the frame was covered with plants and earth. A short hall led to the entrance, which always faced east and the rising sun.

DID YOU KNOW?

If someone died in a hogan, it couldn't be used anymore and was often destroyed.

Like other Native American homes, hogans had an opening in the top to let out smoke from the fire inside.

PIT HOUSES

A pit house is just what it sounds like: a house built in a deep pit, with half of it below the surface of the ground. This type of house was found in California and in parts of Washington, Oregon, Idaho, and Montana.

The pit house had a log frame. The walls and roof were covered with grass, sticks, bark, and other plant matter, and then covered with earth. As was usually the case, there was a smoke hole in the roof.

DID YOU KNOW?

You entered a pit house through a hole in the top and climbed down a ladder to get to the floor!

In some places, pit houses might be connected by tunnels that people could use during cold, snowy winters.

PLANK HOUSES

Native peoples of the Northwest Coast built plank houses. These houses got their name because they were made of planks, or boards, tied to wooden frames.

The Northwest Coast area is full of towering red cedar trees, and the Native Americans used these to build their homes. The homes were huge, up to 60 feet (18 m) wide and 150 feet (46 m) long. They had no windows, but planks in the roof could be moved to let light in.

DID YOU KNOW?

In summer, native peoples of the Northwest Coast left their homes to go to villages for fishing. They removed the planks from their houses and took the planks with them!

Several families lived in each plank house.

IGLOOS

You've likely heard of igloos. Some Inuit in the Arctic chose to live in homes of snow.

Men built the igloos. It took two men several hours to build one. They had to choose the snow carefully—it couldn't be too hard or too soft. Women and children filled in holes and spaces between the blocks of snow. A tunnel-like entrance led into the igloo. There was a "window" of clear ice above the tunnel and a small air hole in the roof.

DID YOU KNOW?

Some Arctic peoples lived in homes that were more like pit houses. But the frame was made from whale bones instead of wooden posts!

WHERE NATIVE AMERICAN HOMES ARE FOUND

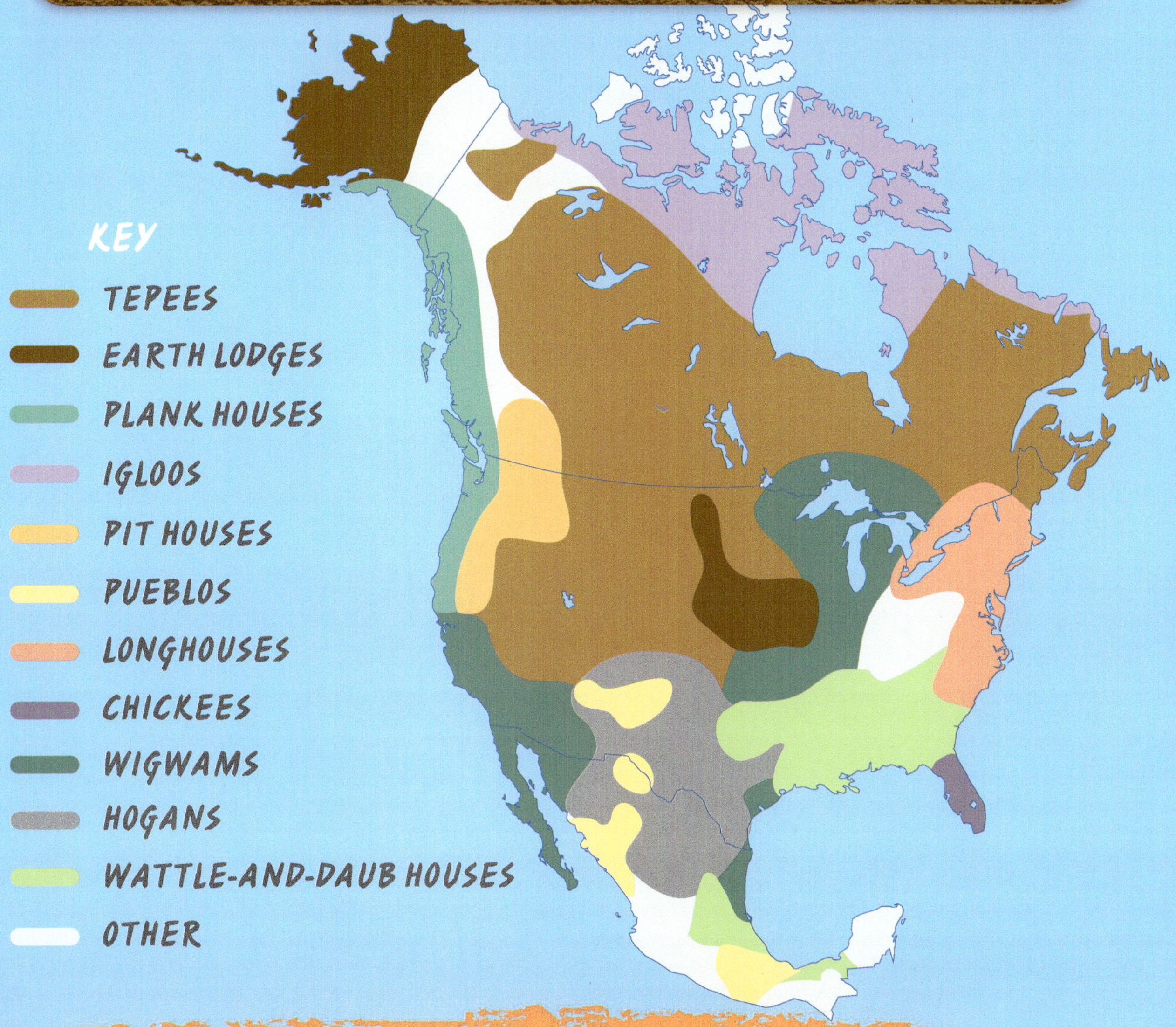

There were even more types of homes than this. Native Americans were creative with the natural resources around them!

NATIVE AMERICAN HOMES TODAY

Today, most Native Americans live in the same kinds of homes you and your friends do. However, some still choose **traditional** housing. Some families in the Southwest live in the same pueblos their **ancestors** lived in long ago. Some Navajo **elders** prefer to live in hogans.

Otherwise, traditional houses are built only for special events or for special purposes such as meeting halls. If you could live in one type of traditional Native American home for a while, which kind would you choose?

Most Native Americans today live in modern houses and apartments like this.

GLOSSARY

adobe: bricks made of clay or earth dried in the sun

ancestor: a person in past times who is in someone's family

celebrate: to honor with special activities

chalk: a soft, white or gray stone

elder: an older person honored for their wisdom

natural resource: something in nature that people can use

nomadic: having to do with people who move from place to place

shallow: not deep

shelter: a place that keeps one safe

traditional: having to do with long-practiced ways of life

vine: a plant that is not strong enough to hold itself up, but climbs over objects or other plants

weave: to make something by passing materials back and forth and over and under each other

wetland: land that has a lot of water in the soil and is usually covered with water at least part of the year

FOR MORE INFORMATION

BOOKS

Flynn, Riley. *Plank Houses*. North Mankato, MN: Capstone Press, 2015.

Manning, Jack. *Tepees*. North Mankato, MN: Capstone Press, 2015.

Williams, Colleen Madonna Flood. *Homes of the Native Americans*. Philadelphia, PA: Mason Crest, 2014.

WEBSITES

Native American Dwellings
mrnussbaum.com/native-american-dwellings/
Find information on Native American homes here, along with photos and videos.

Native American Homes in Olden Times
nativeamericans.mrdonn.org/homes.html
Read more about different types of Native American homes and how they were built.

INDEX